Maria Valleetsy

The Dark Room

First things first:

Here's what BDSM actually stands for:

BDSM includes bondage and discipline (B&D), dominance and submission (D&S), and sadism & masochism (S&M). The terms are lumped together that way because BDSM can be a lot of different things to different people with different preferences, BDSM writer and educator Clarisse Thorn, author of The S&M Feminist, tells BuzzFeed Life. Most of the time, a person's interests fall into one or two of those categories, rather than all of them

Prologue

Immerse yourself in a sensual world of seductive passion brought to life in this enchanting masterpiece. This book will captivate you with its captivating story that magically combines the ardent lust, burning desire and surrendered devotion.

The words in this work are carefully chosen to awaken your senses and set your imagination ablaze. With provocative descriptions, it takes you to the depths of human desire and makes you feel the tingling eroticism on every page.

Only for those who have the courage to explore the boundaries of eroticism and discover their hidden desires, this book is made. It is a work that will appeal to your most intimate dreams and ignite your deepest desires as you plunge into the dangerously tantalizing vortex of passion.

The Dark Room

The house is located on a small hill in the middle of a forest that surrounds the village. As perfect as the idyll seems with all its lakes, hills and forests, if you take a look at the large gray property on the small hill, the new, foreign comfort disappears and changes into a tingling feeling that drives everyone back into the center of the village. The house is surrounded by a large front garden that looks more like a jungle. On closer inspection, the old building is most reminiscent of a princely villa from the 18th century with all its advantages and disadvantages.

Once you have managed to get through the garden to the large wooden double doors, you look in vain for the bell in the gray brickwork.

However, a steel metal ring replaces this in an incredibly romantic way.

The two-story house leaves enough space for more than two people in love. Via the entrance hall you can reach the second floor via the spiral staircase where the bedrooms and guest rooms are located. Of course, the interior design of the villa is customized. Large portraits with decorated wooden frames decorate the walls, whose eyes always seem to be following you.

The large candle wall holders let you feel the medieval austerity but at the same time enchant you with their outgoing warmth.

The tables, chairs and cupboards made of dark red wood do not allow the warmth and comfort to evaporate so quickly.

But just as the villa is out of the context of the small village, something here in the villa is out of the ordinary.

My life here has become almost cliché. After leaving my parents' house and moving in with my current husband, I've been spending almost 10 years behind the stove and looking after the house. But it's not that I'm unhappy. I have found

my place and I am not tormented by boredom here.
Even though I often have to do without my husband because of my frequent business trips, I am never alone here.
In contrast to my husband, I am quite a petite person. At almost 1.66 m, I'm not exactly tall.
Without being vanity, I can say that I am quite slim.
I am just as proud of my slim waist and my flat stomach as I am of my small, delicate breasts, which are adorned with small, long nipples.
However, you will find out more if you read my story.

Friday:
It's Friday again. All the work is done and I can collapse, exhausted, on the four-poster bed.
Flattered by the warm summer sun shining on me through the large windows, I quickly regain my energy and go over my work schedule again in my head.
I've been waiting for a weekend together for so long. It's been a week since I haven't seen him.
There's already a knock on the door.
The sound of the knocking metal ring caused a tingling sensation all over my body. Instead of calmly going to the door like I always did, I stood

up in a flash and, with shaking knees, quickly went down the stairs to open the door.
There he stood in front of me. The dark silhouette of his coat in the sunshine made my heart stop for a second. I immediately threw my arms around his neck and showered him with kisses. I was shocked to realize that a tear of joy was running down my cheek.
He showed up punctually as always with a small smile on his face. My husband and master.
In order not to suffocate him, I reluctantly let go and took a step back to present myself.
I had dressed up for him especially for this day. A short red fabric dress with thin straps and a wide neckline, my privates were only covered by a thong, which was supposed to drive away my tiredness from the long journey.
His eyes told me that I had probably succeeded.
Without a word, I took him by the hand and led him into the living room where the food was already ready.
Exhausted, he put down his bag and coat and disappeared into the bathroom to freshen up briefly.
His lack of words made me suspicious, as he had never been so quiet before.
When he came back, I asked quietly what he had planned for today. However, received no response.

"Let's eat first. "I'm hungry," he said firmly.
Time didn't seem to pass and I was already thinking about why he was so dismissive. I kept noticing his eyes sliding along my body.
When the last drop of wine had been emptied in the glass, he stood up, took my hand and told me to go to the cellar. His voice told me that a contradiction or a question would result in severe punishment.
My split personality, as I call it, turned to its hidden side.
However, I didn't give it any further thought and quickly left.
Behind the steel door was a world of its own. A world in which all feelings existed.
Once you managed to open the door, you looked out onto a seemingly endless black hallway.
However, a small white light switch brings some light into the oppressive darkness and you can see a large room with two steel cupboards, a couch and some, for a layman, indefinable objects. In the corners of the ceiling there are red and black fluorescent tubes that cast an interesting light into the room.
On the wall there is a large St. Andrew's cross with hand and ankle cuffs at the ends. A black leather trestle decorates the middle of the room, with the

ankle cuffs creating a cramped feeling just by looking at them.

Two pairs of handcuffs attached to a chain stick out on the other wall.

A few other objects are covered with a white cloth and shine through the black light.

In the right corner there is a small corridor that leads to a kind of toilet. It only contains a sink, a toilet and a small bathtub.

The red light gives everything a warm glow that triggers the wildest feelings in me.

With my head bowed, I stood in front of the large steel door and waited for my gentleman, who appeared a few minutes later with a suitcase.

I shifted nervously from one foot to the other. The butterflies in my stomach seemed to tear me apart.

The door slowly opened and I looked into the room in awe. When the door slammed loudly, I jumped and hugged my master for protection.

He grabbed my bottom roughly with his hand and pushed me forward.

"It's been a week since we were last here. And I bet you weren't in here alone," I heard him say.

"No, sir, I can't open the door by myself. "You weren't there either and I have no business being here alone," I said with a trembling voice.

When he said that today would be one of my toughest weekends, a chill ran down my spine. But he didn't dare ask what he meant by that.
Excited, I kept looking carefully at his suitcase, which he usually never has with him.
But before I could form another thought, the next command was waiting for me.
"Take off your clothes and go to the bathroom, you're not clean!"
Offended, I pulled down the two straps and let the dress fall to the floor. I immediately got goosebumps which increased to the point of trembling. The thong disappeared with it.
His hard, demanding manner, which I loved so much, quickly made my crack wet, which made it even more uncomfortable to stand there completely naked.
He told me to bend over the edge of the bathtub and relax.
From the other room I heard the squeaking metal door of the closet.
I eagerly tried to see what he was holding in his hands when he entered the toilet.
In a calm voice he made it clear to me that I needed to relax and not be afraid of what was about to happen.
Fearfully, I ask what he's planning to do and what he has in his hands.

But received no answer.
He knew exactly my fear of unknown things. But I also knew how to deal with it.
Suddenly I felt his warm hand rubbing my back, which made me purr pleasantly. His hand continued down my butt to my labia. He carefully opened it with his finger and slowly slid his index finger into me. A slight moan escaped me when I realized how wet I had already become.
He massaged my clitoris and rubbed my juice all the way to my butthole, which he continued to work with his finger.
Without being surprised, I enjoyed the beautiful feeling and closed my eyes as he penetrated my back entrance with two fingers.
The pleasant tingling sensation that arose made the cold disappear from my body and the first beads of sweat formed on my back.
When my moans got louder, he immediately pulled his fingers out and reached for the container of Vaseline that he had brought from the closet. He rubbed it on my anus, which was still slightly open, and penetrated briefly again. The warm, slippery feeling created a pleasant feeling that almost drove away my fear.
I opened my eyes in shock when I suddenly heard water running. However, my unfortunate position

did not allow me to see what my master was doing.

After a short while I felt a kind of tube entering my bottom. I winced when I felt the cold rubber. But before I could protest, he calmed me down with his voice and ordered me to keep quiet.

He backed away from me and took something out of the suitcase again.

You will now have a small initial enema and then another one that will fill you completely!"

Those words scared me more than anything in the world.

"Why are you doing that?" I then dared to ask.

"It will be a new experience for you. It will be the beginning of a long ordeal that will make us much richer!"

I felt like I was going to faint from fear. I had already been through so much. I melted with mixed emotions. He was the first man who lived out my submissive disposition with me and led me on new paths.

I slowly noticed how warm water was flowing into me. After a short while I felt a cramp in my stomach. As the pain increased, I tried desperately to hold it back and breathe it away.

When he noticed that I was having difficulty with the water, he reached between my legs and massaged my stomach.

After a short time that no longer helped and begged for an end. His silence told me that there was no end in sight.

I panicked. I lay helpless over the edge of the bathtub and was mercilessly at the mercy of my master.

"So, that was 1 ½ liters," he said and turned off the water.

Breathing heavily, I thank him for saving me. But he didn't think about getting out of my misery.

He turned away and came back with something black.

"I will give you the butt plug as a stopper for as long as possible so that nothing squirts out of you!"

I had already had to get used to it, so I could breathe a sigh of relief at first. The water inside me slowly spread and became more bearable.

The slippery sound told me that he was rubbing the butt plug with Vaseline and carefully pulling the rubber tube out of me. However, the anal plug came with unusual speed and I tensed up, which caused me pain.

However, my master's satisfied hum made me quickly forget about it. Nothing was nicer than satisfying my master.

When the tension was almost unbearable, the saving order came.

Emptying!
He slowly pulled the stopper out of me. My butt hole must have been so stretched by now that I was afraid I wouldn't let all the water out beforehand.
I squeezed it with all my strength and jumped onto the toilet, which luckily was right next to me.
A wide jet must have sprayed out of me. A disgusting noise that immediately made my face blush. I always had my privacy in such transactions.
When everything was out of me after 10 minutes, the horrible thought of another enema occurred to me.
My hope that he might have forgotten was confirmed by his harsh order to immediately put me back in the old position. My initial hesitation was immediately punished with a slap on my butt. To avoid another one, I quickly bent over the edge of the bathtub again.
The procedure began again. This time, however, I caught a glimpse of the large bottle he was holding in his hand. This time, however, it was full. The 2 liter mark was reached.
Again I noticed the gelled rubber hose. I coped well with the first liter.
Another cramp bothered me, but it was relieved by further massages.

Soon the feeling that I had to burst came back again. The pressure inside me seemed to be endless and with a tormented expression and breathing heavily I kept asking him to stop.
No reaction.
He ran his hand over my back again, all the way to my cunt, where he carefully worked the labia with his fingers.
When he finally lightly penetrated me with two fingers, I was shocked to see how wet I had become. If my body wasn't so heated, I would certainly be able to notice the mucus running down my legs.
After another agonizing minute that seemed like an eternity, I felt the tap turn off. I couldn't help but gasp in pain at that moment. I was shocked to look at my bloated stomach, which had become huge. I squeezed my bottom tightly again when I noticed that my master was slowly moving the plug over my crack to my butt hole. This time, however, the pressure was too much and some of the water sprayed out of me. I quickly closed my eyes out of fear of the impending punishment.
But nothing happened.
Pushing the plug in so quickly made my butthole burn like fire. It's hard for me to hold back tears in this situation.

After an eternity I was allowed to empty myself, which made that disgusting noise again. He stood still in the corner and watched me with a small grin on his lips.

"Now that you're apparently clean, let's move on to the next stage!"

After his brief disappearance, he came back with a dog collar.

"You will wear this this weekend unless I tell you otherwise. You're not allowed to do anything else!"

I silently lowered my head and let him put the leather strap on. It didn't look so bad after all. It had a nice thick leather strap with a silver chain on it.

The still cold leather wrapped tightly around my neck.

A tug on the chain and my knees landed on the ground. Another tug on the leash made it all too clear to me that I should follow him as quickly as possible.

In my humiliating position, I followed my master like a bitch.

As I left the toilet, I was hit by a cool breeze that showed me how wet I really had become.

He was now standing in the middle of the room and instructed me with his gaze and his finger that I should now quickly go to the couch.

Since my knees were already slightly sore, I quickly crawled onto the soft couch and let myself fall into a comfortable and at the same time provocative position.

I lay there for probably a quarter of an hour and didn't move.

He just stood there and looked at me.

Then he took a deep breath and ordered me to kneel on my stomach. Just like I had taught. I crawled off the couch on all fours and assumed the commanded position in front of him so that he could get a good look at my butt hole.

He gently stroked my back opening again and massaged it lightly. After a while he went into the toilet and got the forgotten can of lubricant. He came behind me and lubricated my butthole extensively from the outside and inside. He carefully penetrated me with two fingers, then three, to slowly stretch me. My last anal satisfaction was a long time ago. I clearly noticed the tension in my anus, which, as my master knew, gave me great pleasure. The pleasant tingling sensation spread from my anus to my pussy and caused violent contractions in my abdominal area. He slowly pulled his fingers out of me and I could clearly feel how my butthole remained open for a short time. However, he ignored this and jerked me up with my chain and sucked me towards the buck.

Stumbling, I leaned over him. My master locked the ankle cuffs that made escape impossible. He conjured up a black cloth from somewhere and blindfolded me with it. The fact that I couldn't see anything left me feeling insecure. However, taking a deep breath brought me inner peace again. Suddenly I noticed how his warm hands slowly moved up my thighs.

The idea of being able to feel his entire masculinity inside me drove me crazy and a big breath of air made it clear to me that my body had never been more ready to receive him.

With two fingers he opened my cunt from which a gush of cunt slime ran out. I could already feel his big glans between my bottom. He pulled it down a little and slowly penetrated my hot opening. He started thrusting me slowly and deeply. In all the way and almost all the way out.

The whole situation had me so turned on that after just a few minutes my body gave in and convulsed with a violent orgasm. But my master was far from finished. He grabbed me from behind and tweaked my nipples, which were already stiffly sticking out from me.

His thrusts became harder and my moans became louder and sharper. It was a wonderful feeling to have his cock so deep inside me. My gaping cunt greedily took him in again and again only to release him again a short time later. I savored every thrust as if it were the last.

He pulled him out of me all at once. Was I so in a trance that I didn't notice his orgasm?

I realized that he wasn't finished yet when he inserted a finger into my butt hole and slowly stretched it. He stepped back a little and pressed his glans against my still closed one

Anus. The pressure became more and more intense and I cramped more and more. My face turned red again. There had never been any problems when he wanted to penetrate my butt hole.

He stopped and slowly ran his hand over my mons pubis and rubbed my mucus all the way to my butthole.

He started again. This time it worked. He slowly pushed his cock into my anus, deeper and deeper deeper that I'm gasping for air to stay relaxed. He began with slow thrusting movements that became increasingly stronger.

He reached around me again and tweaked my nipples. He squeezed her harder and harder. The pain increased and I felt like I was going to tear. But he seemed to notice and slowly pulled it out of me. I had the feeling I could feel every single vein.

Due to the violent stretching, my butt seemed to have remained open, because before I knew it I felt his tongue on my butt cheek, approaching my anus in circular movements. Since I had never had anything like this before, I tried to stay calm as new waves of pleasure kept coming over me and making my body twitch. And his tongue had already reached my center and was circling it, his two hands pulled my buttocks apart and he penetrated me with his tongue and satisfied me with thrusting movements. I lost my composure and moaned loudly, the feeling became more and more intense and the orgasm was steadily approaching. Seconds before my anal climax, he flicked his tongue out and pushed his powerful cock back into my pussy and immediately started thrusting hard.

I soon noticed how his glans began to twitch wildly and he poured a huge load into me. When he pulled it out of me, I felt his warm sperm running down my legs and goosebumps spread across my back.

I stayed on the box for a while and slowly gained new energy. I don't know how long. Since entering the room I had lost all sense of time. After a while my master also seemed to have recovered. He slowly came towards me and rubbed my back and stood behind me. Testing, he stuck a finger into

my leaking hole, leaned over me and stuck his cum-covered finger into my mouth, which I quickly sucked clean. He backed away and opened my ankle cuffs. But he immediately grabbed me again and dragged me on the leash towards the bathroom.
In a strong voice he ordered me to bathe as quickly as possible and opened the tap.
After a short time, enough water had come in and I got into the bathtub and washed myself.
My master had already made himself comfortable on the couch in the main room and was waiting for me there. After the quick cleaning, I walked over to him, stark naked and with my head bowed, and knelt in front of him. He threw the clothes that were lying on the backrest onto the floor and ordered me to get dressed and follow him.
I quickly slipped the dress over me and took the thong in my hand. He stood up and dragged me behind him by the chain I was still wearing.
We left the dark room and went back to the shared bedroom.
Once there he took off my necklace, gave me a gentle kiss and disappeared into the bathroom. When he came back, he was already in his pajamas and was slipping my straps off his shoulders. Again I stood naked in front of him. After a quick

inspection, he took my hand and brought me into bed with him.

"I hope you enjoyed the evening. You had to go through a lot today, but you survived it all bravely. It continues tomorrow. "But sleep now, my darling," I heard him whisper. He gave me a kiss and I fell into a deep sleep.

Saturday:
The morning light shining through the half-opened red curtains woke me early from my sleep. A glance to the side told me that my master was not impressed by the incident light.
I wondered with pleasure what he was dreaming about and what he planned to do with me today. I still felt like I was his slave. Yesterday evening made this all too clear to me.
In order to do justice to my new role, I groped into the kitchen, still a little sleepy, to prepare breakfast and bring it to my master in bed.
Within a few minutes the tray was full of delicious things that were supposed to make him wake up easier and make him proud of me. You could smell the delicious warm smell of the rolls that were still in the oven all the way into the bedroom.
I carefully walked into the room with the full tray and placed it on the floor with my feet. Suddenly the clock rang - rolls ready.

When I returned with the full bowl of rolls, my master had already woken up and was rubbing the sleep from his eyes. When he saw the breakfast tray, he smiled at me and, with a wave of his hand, took me to bed with him. Gave me a deep kiss and thanked me for the nice gesture. But I won't spare you because of that, were just the following words.

His first roll, which he spread with honey, quickly disappeared into his mouth. The second one didn't stay on the plate for long either.

I looked at him for a while, amazed at his great appetite. I didn't know why, but I suddenly felt wet. Since I was still lying naked next to him the whole time, it didn't stay a secret for long. He looked at me in surprise, but didn't react any further and continued to concentrate on breakfast.

I became more and more nervous and shifted around on the blanket. When I couldn't take it anymore, I carefully reached under his blanket, looking for his cock.

Don't take your eyes off him so that you can react correctly to every reaction he makes. When I finally had him in my hand, I didn't hesitate for long and started rubbing him carefully and massaging his testicles gently. He still gave no reaction, no word, no smile.

My desire increased so much that I put my head under the blanket to feel his manhood in my mouth. My warm tongue slowly stroked from bottom to top. A quiet clatter told me that he was putting the tray on the floor. Suddenly he pulled the blanket away and watched me enjoy my comedy. To make things even more interesting, I reached over to the tray and took the spray cream that was actually there for the coffee and sprayed his glans with it. My tongue greedily darted out again and licked the cream. My entire mouth was now filled with his cock and cream. I gently began to suck the first drops of juice out of him. Abruptly he pulled me up and sank his shaft into my crack with a pop. Startled by the speed, I groaned loudly and pressed my lips to his mouth and gave him a small amount of cream and his own juice, which probably made him even more excited. Again and again he thrust hard and pulled it almost all the way out only to push it in again with full hardness. I liked the hard game more and more from moment to moment and gave me an even stronger climax that I screamed out loud. Unlike usual, I slipped off him to take his slimy cock back into my mouth. The taste of my own juice made me hornier again and I sucked harder and harder on his glans, which was already starting to pulsate. A few more flicks of his tongue and he unloaded his warm sperm into my mouth, which I tried to swallow as quickly as possible. When I wanted to lick the last bits from the corner of my mouth, he pulled me back to him and did it himself.

I looked at him in surprise, but was happy about this unprecedented perversion. He just sat back with a smug smile.

Bathed in sweat, I hopped out of bed and disappeared into the shower. In the hot shower I noticed that my butt hole was still a little irritated. I probably completely forgot about time under the roaring water, because when I dried myself there was only a piece of paper and a black box on the bathroom cabinet.

"See you in the dark room, slave!"

In the box was the dog collar with the chain that I already knew.

I quickly dried myself, put on the thong and bra and strapped the harness on. With a hasty step and a butterflies in my stomach that threatened to tear me apart, I went down the stairs and through the dark hallway. As I headed down the path of perversion, the wildest thoughts flashed through my mind.

I stopped before I entered the threshold of the room. Took another deep breath and entered the room, which was flooded with neon lights.

He was sitting on the couch that I walked straight towards. I walked towards him with my chest out and my head lifted. When I stood a meter in front of him, he slowly stood up and came behind me. Tense, I closed my eyes and waited for a reaction.
Pat! "Auh" A burning pain spread across my bottom.
Zack! "Uughh" A second hard slap, on the other butt cheek.
I tried tensely to suppress the burning pain.
"Kneel, slave!"
At the command my heart burst and I almost fell to my knees on my own.
Two more slaps on my bottom and a tear ran down my cheek.
Even after thinking about it for a long time, I couldn't answer the question of what I did wrong.
"What did I say about your attitude and dress code?" he asked in a frightening voice. But before I could answer, he threw the crop on the floor next to me and leaned over me. He firmly grabbed the back of my head and pulled it back. With his other hand he placed a gag ball in my mouth. He tied the buckle at the back of his head tightly and began to slowly inflate the rubber ball. He looked me in the eyes coldly and with a small grin.
This tight feeling made my knees tremble. The ball was getting bigger and bigger and was already

filling my entire mouth. I could never have imagined that I would be made his slave at this very moment. How far he would take it was still unclear to me.

My tongue had already been pushed back so far that I could only signal with a moan that I was at the end.

He grabbed my left arm and pulled me up. My bottom was still burning, but he didn't seem to care. He dragged me to the handcuffs that hung from the ceiling with a steel chain and finally chained me. He just stood in front of me and took off my underwear. I now stood there, completely exposed, with my arms outstretched. When he pulled a mask out of his black monk's habit and pulled it over my head so that my entire head was covered and I could no longer see anything, I prayed that this would all be over quickly. I no longer saw anything, I heard almost nothing more and I could no longer ask for mercy. It was quiet for quite a while. I just hung there and hoped for the best.

I jumped when I suddenly felt his hand on my anus. He smeared it again with cream and now and then penetrated it with a finger to make it slippery on the inside.

He whispered something quietly, but couldn't understand it. I just hoped he didn't demand an answer from me.
Suddenly this cold rubber hose entered me again and I felt the lukewarm water flow into me. My stomach clenched every now and then, but I had gotten used to that by now. When the water stopped flowing after a short while, I wondered if it was less water this time or if he was trying to spare me from the cramps. He then slowly pulled the hose out of me and immediately put the anal plug back in.
Quietly.
It wasn't until a few minutes later that I felt something on my knees. I immediately recognized the cold leather tip of the crop.
He slowly moved it higher, which gave me goosebumps that I won't soon forget. However, the strange feeling of being filled with water and this rubber part all the time didn't go away.
A shiver of lust, fear and discomfort came over me as he ran the tip of the crop up the inside of my thigh and slowly approached my labia.
When he drove the leather strap between them, I had to surrender to the warm, pleasant shiver and winced once. Still didn't see what was happening around me. At that moment I no longer knew

whether I would have asked him to stop if I had been able to talk.

Now he ran the tip over my pubic mound all the way to my bloated stomach. The warm tingling sensation accompanied the tip like a star trail accompanying a shooting star. He circled all the way to my nipples, which he lovingly played around and then made them erect with light strokes. The slight pain became a pain of pleasure that I humbly accepted. Suddenly he let go of me again and there was silence around me again.

He let go of me and crept around me, eyeing me. I immediately tried to assume a dignified posture and pushed my chest out and my stomach in. Stretching out my bottom caused me some problems because the plug was quite large and uncomfortable.

His constant nodding told me that I was probably doing everything right, which gave me joy.

He turned away again and got something out of the cupboard and it became dark around me. He used the pulley to pull my arms up so that he could really see everything about me that he wanted. Out of shame and fear, I closed my eyes and hoped nothing worse would happen.

The gurgling in my stomach was getting louder and louder, but I had already gotten used to the strange feeling and almost didn't notice it anymore.

I jumped when I felt his warm hand on my stomach. He stroked it slowly, but was very gentle and I could almost feel his satisfaction. He began to squeeze his bloated stomach a little, which caused strong pressure in the intestines. I tried bravely to withstand the increasingly tight pressure. When he started kneading my stomach roughly, I couldn't take it anymore and tried to avoid him. He immediately let go of me.

He continued to stroke my wet pussy lips, which he gently caressed. He grabbed my thighs and spread them wide apart. Suddenly I felt a foreign body on my clit but didn't dare open my eyes. It was slippery and even felt pleasant.

Slowly a tingling sensation arose inside me and I noticed how I was becoming looser and how my juice was being distributed between my labia. He drove the thing further down and finally penetrated me.

"So," he said, "I always want to see one of your holes filled, if not you will be punished."

Even though the dildo-like thing inside me seemed pretty big, it didn't hurt.

I hung there for a while and was at the mercy of my master's probing touches. After his examination, he took me off his hands and led me to the toilet, where he slowly took out my butt plug and I was allowed to empty myself. This empty feeling didn't stay with me for long. He started fingering my butthole again with his creamed fingers. He penetrated me more often than usual with several fingers and this time he also used his second hand to help pull my butthole apart.

When the pain became too much, I couldn't help it and started moaning. Smack, I immediately received a slap on my bottom with the palm of my hand. "It's true today, if you can't take it anymore, don't complain anymore, but say: Mercy, Lord!",

"Understood?"

"Yes, sir," I managed miserably.

After a short hum, he turned his attention to my butt again and this time slowly pushed his finger in and out again. I slowly inserted the tip of the plug and slowly screwed it in. This time it was easier for me to take it in, although it was still a lot of pressure and extremely uncomfortable.

He jerked me up by my collar and walked me back into the main room. The cold air that flowed towards me made me shiver, which made the already cumbersome walking even more difficult. Half stumbling, I was pulled onto the long bench where my master let me sit down. He grabbed my shoulder and pushed me down firmly. I was now more or less comfortable on the bench, which was far too short, so that only my legs hung down a little. I was still shaking all over. A wave of cold but also unknown pleasure overcame my body, making my fine hairs stand up noticeably. Once again I could hardly see anything going on around me when suddenly something liquid ran down my back. Something warm and oily quickly collected in the hollow of my back. His warm hands gently massaged my entire back, shoulders and a small part of my upper arm. They gently slid further down my spine to massage my bottom, where some of the oil was applied again. The few gentle touches quickly gripped my soul, causing me to sob deeply. After a short while, he grabbed my pelvis and pulled me further back with my bottom, which made me raise my pelvis further. The massage started again, allowing me to relax further and pushing away my thoughts about what bad things my master might have in store for me. His soft hands slowly slipped deeper and deeper and I enjoyed a wonderful pubic massage. Occasionally one or two fingers slipped into me and stimulated me incredibly strongly, so that within a short time some of my juice came out and apparently dripped down.

He gently let go of me and turned away. The squeaking doors of the small cupboard behind me told me that something new was coming. I was still completely relaxed and enjoyed what were probably the last few quiet minutes I had left. Two hands touched my back again and moved slightly in circles down to my pelvis. He gently played around the plug with one hand and kept nudging it lightly and began to turn it slightly, which made me take a deep breath and further aroused me. Slowly he finally pulled it out, my muscle tensing so much that it almost popped out. With his oily hand he massaged my anus and penetrated my intestines again with several fingers, but this time extremely gently.

Suddenly I felt something cold again with what seemed to be a large tip, which was touching my closed butt hole. When it started to press heavily against my hole, the pleasant relaxation disappeared. When he pushed it into me with great force, I couldn't hold myself any longer and let out a scream. At that moment I no longer dared to ask him to stop and endured the tearing pain of the spread muscle. For a moment I thought I was going to tear up, but at the right moment, he was sunk into me to the hilt. Breathing quickly, I realized that it was probably the next level of stretching and tried to calm myself down. Slowly I realized why he allowed me to relax and rest so much.

He stroked my back again and gave me a kiss on the neck, then jerked me up and, even though my knees seemed to be about to give in, stood me up and led me in front of him towards the exit.

The plug seemed to more than completely fill me up and made walking next to impossible, painless almost impossible.

When the seemingly endless corridor came to an end and I was sure of success, I looked at the first staircase.

I stood there helpless.

First a small, then a somewhat violent push forward made it clear to me that he was serious. But I couldn't. That much was clear: I wouldn't be able to do it alone with this thing in my butt. When I didn't go up the stairs after another push, hell came to me. He pushed the plug in forcefully with his finger, which caused hellish twitches and a strange pain. At that moment my knees gave out and I collapsed. However, my master quickly caught me with a grab under the arms and apart from the pain I was more or less fine. "GO slave, I certainly won't carry you up! "So let's go!" he shouted at me.

Still crouching on my knees, I tried to more or less crawl up the stairs. The seemingly endless way up was finally reached and I was now lying at the top of the stairs, sweating and completely exhausted.

I still had a deep breath before he pulled me up by my collar, stabilized me and pushed me forward. This time was it towards the kitchen, or was it the bedroom?

Shaking and swaying, I came to the bedroom where he left me standing in front of the big, soft bed that I longed for more than anything else. The temptation was almost too great to simply let myself fall forward and fall into what I hoped would be a long sleep. But the fear of punishment or great disappointment was too great. He loosened my collar and got rid of his things and I could feel his warmth that my cold body greedily absorbed. He grabbed my arm and pulled me towards the bathroom.

I still hadn't gotten used to the plug and so my gait was still clumsy and clumsy. On the way to the bathroom I caught a quick glimpse of the wall clock whizzing by

throw - 2:40 p.m.!

My personal proof of how long I was down there and in what strange ways time passed.

I almost felt safe up here because nothing was happening in the apartment that reminded me of the grim reality in the dark room. However, before I could think any further, we had arrived in the bathroom and my master obligingly opened the door of the somewhat large shower and, due to the difficulties caused by my predicament, helped me into the shower, which he entered immediately after me.

He quickly turned on the warm water because he was probably cold too. However, he left me with the first warm shower, which quickly caused my temperature to rise back to normal and allowed me to slip back into a state of relaxation despite the plug. However, I stepped aside a little and let my husband also feel the warm shower. After he had quickly warmed up, he carefully grabbed my waist, pulled me close to him, lowered his head and gave me a deep French kiss that was so loving and tender that I almost forgot about the first part of the day He continued to gently kiss my neck and run his hand over my cheeks.

I searched for the shower gel with one hand and then soaped myself up. However, before the first drop of gel could land on my hand, he took the bottle from my hand and dripped some gel onto my breasts, which were then gently lathered. Released from all constraints, I turned around, hoping he would do the same... I already felt the first cool drops of gel on my shoulders, closely followed by his large, soft hands rubbing everything together. He lathered his hands again and carefully reached around my stomach to soap it up in circular movements. His hands kept sliding back and forth, feeling further down my legs and then back up over my mons pubis to my stomach and back to my waist. An unwanted pleasant moan wasn't all that showed my seemingly endless satisfaction. Even his brisk reach between my legs to clean my most intimate area didn't bother me and a tingling sensation in my nipples told me that it was more than satisfaction and relaxation. Helpless in my situation, I stood still for the time being and let it take over, enjoying every second as its preciousness grew more and more. I jumped almost in fear when his hands reached my bottom and moved further down. But nothing happened. He washed my long blonde hair just as lovingly with the shampoo and rinsed it thoroughly so that I didn't have to do anything to get out of the shower completely showered. The plug now caused me fewer problems than before. My husband quickly came after me, quickly grabbed the large bath towel that was hanging over the radiator and was therefore nicely preheated and wrapped it around me.

He carefully dried my body, being careful even in the buttocks region and not causing me any additional pain. After drying himself, he took my hand again and led me towards the bedroom again. He laid me on my stomach and put the blanket over me before putting on fresh clothes and disappearing. Everything happened in such a short time that I closed my eyes exhausted, just let myself go and defined happiness for myself

I was then taken away from my inner conversations by a wonderful smell coming from the kitchen. My first thought was "get up". When I tried, however, I was reminded too quickly of the stopper in me and I left it and imagined the most wonderful dishes in my head when he suddenly stood in the door and had probably been watching me for a while. I couldn't say anything at that moment and so I just looked at him gratefully and lovingly. However, he turned away and opened my wardrobe where, after a short search, he found the pink lace hotpants which he threw on the bed and turned away without a word to disappear back into the kitchen. Should this be a normal day? Without thinking too much about it, I put the panties on and buried myself under the covers again.
Again, quite a while must have passed before the smell became more and more intense and my husband came to my bed with a large tray, but placed it on the dresser and disappeared again. However, a few minutes later he came back with a can. Only when he put it down next to the plate

did I recognize the Nivea cream and my look became more serious. He pulled away the blanket that kept me warm the whole time. I couldn't see his face again, but I knew that something unpleasant would follow. He grabbed my panties and took them off again, I no longer understood the world at that moment, and grabbed my ankles to spread my legs wide. He sat next to me and whispered a lot in my ear. In the excitement I couldn't understand other than that he was sorry. He stroked my bottom and then pulled it apart, which caused slight pangs of pain and the first beads of fear sweat formed. He slowly grabbed the end of the plug and began to twist it slightly. I bit the pillow, even though the pain wasn't too bad, I knew it had to get worse. He began to pull on it slowly, turning it over and over again, so that at some point I screamed and moaned into the pillow. I stubbornly squeezed my eyes shut and tried to relax my muscles as much as possible. Without causing me any further pain, after a few more twists he was out of me and I could breathe a sigh of relief. With a Klinex, which he conjured up from under the bed, he wiped the remaining lubricant from the plug and then carefully applied cream to my sore butthole. Finally, he wiped off the remaining lubricant that was still on my bottom and gave me a kiss on the bottom.

The huge plug that I saw for the first time stood on the table like a threatening memorial. Still lying on my stomach, I got my lace panties back on and the blanket put back on me. I turned around and sat up to eat. Only now that I saw the tray with the wonderful chicken fillet in front of me and took in the smell did I realize how hungry I had been. An eerie feeling of forgetting everything in the basement and only submitting to the Lord.

He was still sitting on the bed and looking at me quietly. I didn't think about it any further and preferred to concentrate on my food. Who knows when I'll next get service like this. I was finished in no time, which I also saw in my little tummy and laughed. He took the tray from my lap and brought it into the kitchen while I made myself comfortable again. The butt plug was still on the dresser and seemed to be staring at me. Just the thought of having him inside me again sent shivers down my spine.

Even though I wanted to get up to move freely again, I was still too exhausted to get up. After a few minutes my husband came back and sat on the bed with me. He leaned over to me again without saying anything and began to caress and massage my breasts, my stomach and finally my labia through my panties. Accompanied by deep French kisses, I quickly became wet, which didn't remain a secret for long thanks to the panties. I started to get nervous when he started stimulating my insides with his finger and pushed myself closer to him, hoping to feel his cock inside me. Despite everything, the kisses became shorter and shorter and his hand withdrew further from moment to moment. Almost offended, I wanted to turn around when he gave me a final kiss and then, with his face almost beaming with glee, I turned around so that I was lying on my stomach again. He slipped off the bed and within a few seconds put my collar around me, came behind me and pulled me back a little so that I was kneeling on all fours on the bed. His hands grabbed the panties again and pulled them down a little so that he had full access to my bottom again. I was almost surprised when he started kissing my bottom and tickling it with his tongue. He penetrated my butt crack more and more determinedly until he finally had his tongue on my anus and tickled it with his tongue. As if in a dark vision, I saw him reach for the plug and the tube of lubricant and before I knew it, the first drops of lubricant were running down my labia. Without warning and without in-depth pre-stretching, he placed the tip and turned quickly, but still with due caution. My butt hole seemed to be tearing and I had the feeling that I had reached the limit. But when I couldn't stand it anymore, I started screaming, which he accepted and continued drilling him. When he got stuck, I tipped over again, but this time I landed softly. I stayed lying there for a moment when my master threw a bathrobe onto the bed and looked at me demandingly. Painfully, I sat up and put him around to make a careful attempt to get up. This time it was much easier for me and I padded over to him, who was already holding the collar chain tightly in his hand. It was more than clear to me where I was going now and my movements became more shaky again, imagining what would await me down there.

The walk down the stairs was much easier, but it still gave me the strangest feelings, not least accompanied by the pain that was pulling at me. The large steel door closed again with a thud. I was amazed at the warm breeze that flowed towards me. When I stood in the middle of the room again, the warm air surrounding me, I immediately felt much more comfortable. The bathrobe, which glowed with the black light, was then taken away from me by my gentleman and the panties, which I was surprised to find, no longer protected my shame. With the collar pulled towards the wall. At that moment I didn't care much about the chains that came out of the wall. My head was still completely numb from the stretching and the various feelings that plagued me today. So I didn't realize what was happening and willingly went after him.

Feeling weak, I let my wrists be tied to the still cold leather straps so I could stand there alone for a few minutes and wait for something. I just stood there quietly. My master had turned away again and was rummaging around in the cupboard. However, he soon came back empty-handed to chain my ankles to the shackles that were further apart.

There I stood now. Legs apart and naked in front of the black wall. There was no movement. A little forward, a little back. Not more.

The plug that continued to spread my butt made it difficult to move anyway, so I didn't have to move much. Looking through the cupboard again, my master came back with a fairly large dildo and something black that I couldn't recognize and turned to me with a smile. My hair was pulled back and he pushed something rubbery into my mouth. A click snapped a clasp into place at the back of my head. A gag order, my first thought. Nevertheless, I was able to open and close my mouth easily. Not a big deal, I thought, and my master began to pump up the strange ball. My eyes opened wide, already unable to speak, I tried to beg for mercy and shook my head wildly.

Nothing.

With each pump, the ball in my mouth grew exponentially to a massive size, forcing my tongue down forcefully and filling my mouth frighteningly. I tried convulsively to breathe quickly through my nose, which caused great difficulty and for a brief moment I almost couldn't breathe. He still looked silently into my eyes for help. I slowly calmed down and tried to breathe normally, which worked after a while and I no longer tensed up.

My master still looked at me wordlessly and stroked my cheek and moved the huge dildo back and forth in front of my eyes. My thoughts immediately turned to my plug, which I didn't want to have pulled out again, even though it would probably be easier for me this time. He gave me another kiss and immediately directed his gaze to my abdomen, which he literally made boil with his gaze. Slowly stroking, he deliberately moved towards my pubic area, which had been more or less spared so far. Without much foreplay, he penetrated me first with one, then two and finally with three fingers and spread the juice from the wetted fingers on the dildo. He can't insert it into me, I wasn't ready for that, that much was clear, but then what does he plan to do with it?

He placed the wet tip of the dildo in circles on my chest and moved it further down again. I closed

my eyes; I couldn't stop anything now. When he started rubbing my clit with the tip, I stood on my tiptoes as best I could. I couldn't say anything, screaming was brutally suppressed. Tears of silent fear streamed down my cheeks at the idea. I began to breathe heavily as he slowly pushed the tip into me, my hole became wider and wider. It quickly reached the point where it seemed like it couldn't go any further. If I had been able to float, I would have reached the ceiling by now, but my toes, which I kept standing on, were too short to escape the torture. Slowly rotating, the red monster drilled into my core and threatened to tear me apart. The skin that separated the intestines and vagina seemed to no longer exist. I imagined that both dildos were touching each other. The veins of the monster that was in my pussy stimulated the stretched labia to such an extent that I became more and more wet, which fortunately made penetration a little easier. Slowly, vein by vein pushed through the taut entrance.
When the burning pain became almost unbearable, I couldn't continue. I was like stiff. Every movement, every fidget would have caused pain.

The violent gasping for air was the only sound I heard. Everything was tugging at me.

The fact of being completely exposed and tormented on the chains didn't make the situation any easier and more tears were shed. After I opened my eyes, which had been closed at the time, I only saw him again, smiling slightly and standing in front of me without saying a word. As I slowly moved from the tips of my toes back to the soles of my feet, an ice-cold shiver ran down my spine and I tried to take a deep breath.
I would have liked to lean against the wall to relieve my legs if it weren't for the other stopper. So I prayed that I would have enough strength to keep me on my feet until the torture was over.
His hands gently touched my inner thighs and slowly moved up from my knees until they reached my crack. Drenched in sweat, I silently longed for the soft bed and the shower. The thought of losing my wonderful tightness through the dildo only came to me later when I had to realize that I would have to forego my bed and rest.
The last tear dried and I had more or less calmed down and faster than I thought my pussy got used to the powerful dildo and after a while the pain almost completely disappeared. His hands were stroking me again and I tried to enjoy it.
He pulled lightly on the erect nipples and squeezed them lightly between his fingers, which made my knees weak.

Unexpectedly, he let go, turned around and left.
Light off.
He was gone.
The last thing I heard was the banging of the door. My head was empty. What happened now? What is he up to? For a long time I just stood there with my legs spread and waited longingly for him to return.

After waiting for what seemed like an endless amount of time, I stopped the door from opening and closing and opened my eyes again. The light flickered in my eyes, which had already gotten used to the darkness.

With my eyes almost closed I see the outline of my master and my eyes opened when I saw the large candle in his hand. He quickly placed it on the trestle and pulled the short bench towards me. He then placed them directly between my legs, a little distance from the wall, and then loosened my ankle and handcuffs. He also removed the mouthguard and I was able to take a deep breath. A few chewing movements brought my condition back to normal and the initially numb feeling in my jaw disappeared. "Lie down carefully on your stomach," his first words since the many hours that must have passed. However, I didn't need to be told twice and carefully lay down on my stomach. However, the dildo made itself felt again in a painful way and I bravely just grimaced.

Now I was lying there with my legs hanging down my sides again. He scratches and lightly tickles me down my neck and up my spine. With his other hand he pulled my butt cheeks apart and started working on the anal plug again. I almost didn't notice the slight twist anymore, but I groaned loudly when he quickly pulled it out. My butthole seemed to still be open as I thought I could feel a breath or two deep inside me.

After he touched me again with his hand, he stood behind me and grabbed my legs. He picked her up and turned them both. One of his gestures that was supposed to make me turn around. I supported myself heavily and turned once so that I was now lying on my back.

He suddenly let go of one leg and I almost had trouble not letting it fall onto the edge of the bench. I was too weak at that moment. Shocked at my own condition, I almost didn't notice a handcuff clamping around my ankle and holding it up. That couldn't have been a kindness. Shortly afterwards the second clamp closed around the other ankle, which spread my thighs wide again and let me feel the dildo deeply again. The nervousness grew by the second. I wanted to scream and run away, my completely open position was too uncomfortable and frightening. With one

hand, he picked up a drinking bottle out of nowhere and took a long drink from it.
I looked at him greedily. Today's tears really took a toll on my water balance.
He in turn just smiled and looked at me.
He lowered the bottle and let some of the cold water drip onto my stomach. A small puddle formed in my belly button and was pleasantly cooling. He let the drops drip further up my sweaty body, causing the nipples to become strongly erect again. I quickly opened my mouth and greedily stuck my tongue at the water that was already splashing on my lips. Finally the releasing rush of water came into my mouth. I almost choked because of my greed. The refreshment didn't last long, because after a few moments the bottle turned away again and the last bit of liquid ran down my breasts and waist onto the floor.
You could see the joy in his eyes as he didn't hesitate to massage a nipple and pinch it.
As if in a bad dream, I saw his hand running down my stomach to my pubic mound and rubbing roughly over the swollen clit, making me wince. He carefully grabbed the dildo and began to slowly twist it out. The veins rubbed against the stretched labia, which made me groan. However, he didn't stop and continued to turn it out little by little. I tried not to show my pain in front of him and

hoped he would praise me for my bravery later and not torture me like that next time. However, my master apparently knew me better than I thought and rubbed my labia with a lot of lubricant so that he could remove the dildo better. He carefully pushed his finger into me and spread the lubricant as best he could. He then slowly pulled and twisted the torture instrument.

When it was finally out of me, I felt her convulsively constrict everything inside me. However, the pain disappeared quickly and I was able to breathe relaxed again. Despite my relatively unbiased position, I still felt trapped and humiliated. I constantly felt an internal burning heat within me. I didn't know whether it was because I was so excited or just because of the torture. For a long time I just lay there and tried to prepare myself for what would await me afterwards. My master left me lying unhindered and was sure to create more torment for me. After a few minutes I heard a splashing noise. My first thought was a refreshing swim. I deserved it the way I had suffered today. I had never been so disciplined before. As it turned out, however, this was just another pipe dream, because just a few moments later there was dead silence again and my master returned. He grabbed my arms roughly and pulled me up to him. Without saying a word he

pulled me behind him. I stumbled after him with shaky legs and followed him to Bad. He placed a tall, large stool in the bathtub and pointed at it.
"Sit there and put your legs over the edge!"
I hesitated for a second, but then quickly sat down. The stool was almost as high as the edge of the bathtub, so my legs were only slightly bent.
My master took a mirror out of a cupboard and attached it to the edge of the tub with a bracket. He grabbed me by my bonds and roughly pulled me further forward and spread my legs further apart. My position was extremely uncomfortable because the stool wasn't exactly softly padded and the edges rubbed against my bottom.
"Look while I work on you!" and pointed to the mirror that was between my thighs. I was shocked when I could see my clearly reddened labia and anus.
"Don't you dare look away!" were his last words before he opened the tap. He ran cool water through the hose over my mons pubis, which was extremely good for me. With one hand he gently massaged my clit. However, when he noticed how my abdomen began to twitch slightly, he stopped immediately.
He attached a kind of small dildo to the blunt end of the hose through which the water now flowed.

Without warning he pushed it into my slime-filled cunt and filled it with the cool water. I was probably already so stretched from the dildo torture that my labia couldn't properly enclose the narrow enema dildo and the excess water could drain away. The redness slowly disappeared and my labia almost returned to their normal color. The cooling water was not only pleasant, it was actually really soothing.

Through the mirror I could watch as my master pulled out my inner labia a little and stretched it a little with one hand. If it weren't for the mirror, I wouldn't have noticed it at all; I was too focused on the cool water.

After a few more moments he pulled the enema dildo out of me and almost recklessly pushed it into my smeared anus. No matter how full he was of lube, he encountered no resistance.

I could see exactly how the muscle closed tightly around the shaft and not a drop of water escaped.

My master probably didn't like that I liked the shower and turned the tap on a little more so that the water filled me quicker. A short time later I clearly noticed how the pressure was building up inside me. My stomach was already noticeably bloated, which my master seemed to like. He spread my pussy lips slightly and inserted his finger

into me and gently massaged my clit with his thumb. Unfortunately only a short relief.
"Watch out! Time to empty!" were his following words.
Without knowing how long I had left until he took the dildo out of me, I immediately tensed my anus as hard as I could, which turned out to be a wise decision. A split second later he pulled it out of me. The pressure was already quite strong within me and I had problems rising from my situation. Even if it was clumsy, I managed it quickly. I was barely sitting on the cold toilet when the water came rushing out of me uncontrollably.
The water shot out of me for a while. Once the jet stopped, it rumbled inside me once and it flowed again. After a while the last drop had dried up and I was allowed to wash downstairs again.
Even though it was still burning a bit downstairs, I felt better than ever.
I was clean.
Inside and outside.
After he checked me again, he seemed happy with me too.
He pushed me from behind and I walked back into his torture chamber with a relieved gait. I was allowed to stand in the middle of the room.
He looked me over briefly from all sides and took off my collar, which made me very relieved.

Because it was a few millimeters too tight, you constantly felt like you were short of breath. Unfortunately, I was happy too soon because he quickly exchanged it for a much wider collar. Luckily, it fit perfectly around my neck and I was able to breathe easily and freely. However, nothing was without disadvantage, and so I was now prevented from tilting my head by the very wide collar.

"So, now to your task."

"I want you to torture yourself now. If you do it well, you will be saved for today. If you fail, I'll take over your task! Do you understand slave?"

Without knowing what to do, I simply nodded.

I didn't know what to do, but I didn't want to disappoint my master. Who knows what punishment I will face then.

I walked around the room on my own and tried to think of something that would make my master happy.

On the table next to the bench there were still some of the dildos and plugs that I had inside me that lunchtime. They were neatly lined up according to size and shape. Luckily, I could now choose the size myself and it seemed to make the most sense to satisfy myself with a small dildo.

I confidently went to the table and wanted the small dildo when my master grabbed me from behind.

"You chose the wrong one!" he said in a stern voice.

Goosebumps ran through me because I was afraid of what was about to happen.

"It's already late and I'll think of a special punishment for tomorrow." He turned away briefly again and came back with two medium plugs in his hands.

"Now go upstairs and take a shower. Afterwards you will insert these two plugs and, as befits a slave, you will do your housework with them. I'll be waiting for you in the bedroom at 6 p.m. for dinner!"

Since I was still stark naked, he allowed me to put a large black cloth around me so that I wouldn't get too cold or catch a cold on the way into the apartment. Despite the warm weather, it was still quite cool in the apartment, especially when you had nothing on.

I breathed a sigh of relief and quickly hurried up the stairs.

Once upstairs, we quickly went into the bedroom. My thoughts were only spinning about the refreshing, cleansing shower that was supposed to delight me in just a few minutes.

I quickly dropped the cloth from my body and put on comfortable underwear and a bathrobe. Seconds later I was standing in the shower and enjoying the warm jet of water that refreshed and warmed me at the same time. I washed my body thoroughly with soap, not neglecting an inch. The entire pelvic area was still smeared with lubricant, which stuck to me like a meal. Only after intensive use of the soap did the gel completely dissolve and I almost felt clean again. The redness on my pussy had now almost completely disappeared and my butthole also felt pleasant again.

After showering for what seemed like an eternity, I spent quite a while applying cream. Back in the bedroom, I started inserting the two plugs. I lay down in the middle of the bed with my legs apart and reached for the tube of lubricant that was on the bedside cabinet. Again I had to apply the greasy cream to my freshly cleaned abdomen. With light pressure I let the first plug slide into my bottom. The plug wasn't extremely thick and I had no trouble picking it up. The second plug also took its place in my pleasure flesh without any complications. I crawled off the bed with a strange gait, took off a bra and put on a bathrobe. With my equipment, panties didn't make much sense. My gait certainly looked strange. With every step I felt the plugs moving inside me. Even though it was a strange feeling, I couldn't deny that it also excited me.

I did my housework to the best of my ability. I washed the dirty dishes, mopped the floors and cleaned the rooms where a lot of dust had collected.

More than three hours had passed when I sat down on the bed, exhausted, after completing my work, and took a deep breath. I was really exhausted and also very hungry.

I heard his footsteps from far away as he went up the first flight of stairs. With every step he took closer towards the bedroom, my excitement increased and a shiver of pleasure ran down my spine like a waterfall. I looked down at myself again to make sure everything was in place. His footsteps became louder and louder and a short time later he was standing in the bedroom door. He looked at me with bored eyes and examined me without changing his expression. Without paying any attention to me, he continued into the bathroom, where he turned on the water and apparently freshened up. Without a word he walked past the bed again, through the door and disappeared.

Disappointed, I tried to understand why he wasn't paying attention to me. However, I couldn't find any flaw in myself. However, I was still too exhausted to follow him and so I just lay there and recovered from the exertion. It took a while for his footsteps to wake me up from my little nap.

When I opened my eyes again, He was already standing in the door. In his hands he held a tray that emanated a delicious smell. My master had made me something to eat.

Of course I was very happy about that and smiled thank you. I immediately assumed an upright position as he placed it on the bed for me. I gave him, albeit a little sleepily, my best smile as a thank you, but his expression was still the same. With a movement of his head that wasn't difficult to interpret, he made it clear to me that the food was for me and that I should kindly empty the tray. After he served me the tray he disappeared again and left me alone. Since I was extremely hungry, I didn't bother with it at first, but started filling my stomach. I greedily gobbled it down and satisfied my growling stomach. However, the plate was emptied all too quickly, but my cravings disappeared and I gave in to my subsequent tiredness. I simply put the plate on the floor and fell back into bed.

I was so exhausted that I quickly fell asleep. For a few hours no one disturbed my peace and so I woke up completely on my own. The sun was already setting outside, turning the sky a beautiful red.

I heard his footsteps again in the distance. I wanted to try again to show him my gratitude and sat down in the middle of the bed. I also opened my bathrobe a little so that he had a clear view of my breasts. I was still wearing my bra, but I knew he particularly liked this one because it was made of a sheer black material that didn't cover a single bit of skin. His footsteps came closer and closer and before I knew it he was standing in the bedroom door. This time, however, he smiled when he saw me and was about to walk past me again, so he sat down on the bed next to me.

"Have you rested, slave?" he asked in a clearly relaxed and gentle voice.

I just nodded and smiled and moved a little closer to him. He pulled my cleavage open a little more to get a better look at my breasts. With a somewhat rough grip he grabbed a breast and kneaded it vigorously. I just kept still and tried to please him. He then opened the bow of the bathrobe and completely exposed me. He spread my legs and made sure I was wearing the two plugs as instructed. He took another deep breath and then got up from the bed. He ran his hands through his hair and quickly got rid of his clothes, which he neatly put aside. He then closed the curtains and came back to bed with me. I was a little disappointed to see that his cock was still hanging limply. Apparently I hadn't aroused him.

He crouched next to me and stripped off my robe and unclasped my bra, throwing them both on the floor next to him.

"Lie flat next to me slave!" he ordered and without having another chance, I slid lower and lay flat on the bed.

My master looked me over carefully, starting from my head, down to my abdomen and thighs and back again. He now ran his hand down my body. He stroked my breasts, my nipples, ran my stomach and finally placed his hand on my shaved pubis. I spread my legs to make myself accessible to him. Apparently I had reacted correctly, because he purposefully worked on the plug that was in my pussy. He began to turn it slightly and tugged at it. It seemed like I kept sucking him back. He repeated it a few more times and then slowly pulled it completely out of me. He repeated the same thing with the other plug. When this was also removed, it felt somehow unusual to be so "empty" again. Testing, he pushed two fingers into my pussy, from which the remaining lubricant ran. Smacking his lips, he pushed it into me as far as it would go, eliciting a soft moan from me.

To my delight, I saw his cock slowly getting bigger and becoming more and more erect. Unfortunately my master finished his finger work much too quickly. After a few strokes he pulled his fingers out and stroked my clit one last time. But something much more wonderful followed. My master knelt between my legs and reached under my pelvis. He grabbed my buttocks with a firm hand and lifted my pelvis towards him. I wanted to accommodate him and bent my legs so that I could keep my pelvis at his level. I could already feel his bulging glans on my labia. Moments later he thrust hard. I moaned shrilly as his cock split my insides. Our abdomens slapped together as he penetrated me deeply again and again. His rhythm became faster and faster, but by no means weaker. His hot hard cock was a pleasure after those stiff rubber dildos. His hands left my pelvis and grabbed my breasts. He held it roughly in his firm hands and kneaded it. It didn't hurt or be uncomfortable at all. I couldn't get enough of his hardness and moaned for more. I always wanted more and hoped it wouldn't stop. My entire body tingled with tension and lust. He pushed into my pussy more and more jerkily and tugged on my breasts. My abdomen began to twitch, first slightly and then more and more violently. I couldn't control it anymore and an incredible orgasm ripped through my body from top to bottom. I groaned loudly in a daze.

For a moment I thought my master had stopped, but seconds later I felt his powerful thrusts again. Completely out of breath, I could only make short, choppy sounds. Although my strength was increasingly failing me and I could only keep my pelvis upright with difficulty, I kept begging for "more". I didn't know where this insatiability came from. Maybe the plugs I wore half the day brought out this greed in me. Moments later my master let go of my breasts and pushed my abdomen down onto the bed. For a brief moment he stopped his penetration and placed his full weight on me. Breathing deeply, he thrust hard again and pressed his lips to my mouth. Just as forcefully as he fucked me, his tongue pushed into my mouth and met mine. I clamped my legs tightly around his body and pulled him even closer to me. If he didn't pin my arms to the bed with his hands, I would hold on to him even more. His cock slid out of my pussy more and more often and then thrust hard again. My abdomen would bulge every time. It was torture not being able to moan and greedily asking for "more". In a split second I felt his cock start to twitch and a massive gush of sperm poured into me. He pushed into my dripping cunt one last time. She also lost her strength and he slipped off me. With his cock I clearly felt the mixture of sperm and my juice running out of my hole. I was still hungry for more and I leaned to the side and closed my lips around his smeared glans. It tasted like pure lust and I greedily licked his softening cock clean and wildly swallowed the pleasure juice. Satisfied, I then fell back on my side and breathed deeply in and out. I would have liked to have let him take me even further. But I didn't dare ask him. I knew he wouldn't like it if his slave asked for more. I left it at that and licked my lips, which were covered in pleasure juice, one last time and closed my eyes.

Sunday:
Still happy from last night, it wasn't difficult for me to wake up. Like every morning, the bright rays of sunlight made their way through the window directly onto me.
Blinking, I adjusted to the bright light. My master had disappeared again, but his smell, the heavy male scent, was in the air, mixed with our smell from the previous night, which brought refreshing memories to me again. I rolled over again comfortably and hopped out of bed. I stretched with pleasure one last time and quickly went into the shower and let the cold, clear water flow down me. I quickly soaped myself, after all I wanted to be

fresh and clean for my master. He should be proud of his slave, and I was also sure that he would punish me if I didn't appear well-groomed.

My stomach growled considerably, interrupting my train of thought.

I quickly finished my shower and slipped into fresh underwear and put on the collar. Everything as I was told. Today I chose the slightly transparent underwear especially for him to entice him to pamper me again like he did last night.

Once everything was ready, I made my way to the kitchen to satisfy my hunger. It was nice and warm throughout the house, so I didn't feel cold even in my skimpy clothes. On the way, I hoped that my master might even have served me breakfast, as he often did. But when I opened the kitchen door I was proven wrong. - Nothing was prepared or prepared. However, my hunger didn't leave me much room for disappointment and I grabbed some eggs and milk from the fridge to make scrambled eggs. The pan was once again hidden in the back cupboard, but when I bent down to pull it out I discovered IT.

IT, was under the table.

Two stainless steel bowls with a yellow Post-It note.

"As of this morning, the slave is no longer allowed to eat like ordinary people.

This is enough for you.
Don't you dare refill it
Don't you dare use cutlery.
Don't you dare move the food bowls from their place.
I'll wait for you in the basement afterwards! Immediately!"
A cold shiver ran down my spine. I turned around to check whether he wasn't standing in the doorway laughing and making a little joke.
Nobody was in the door.
However, the bitter seriousness with which this message was written did not make it look like fun.
So I crawled under the table on all fours and took a closer look at the two bowls.
Milk in one hand and chopped bread and a small diced apple in the other.
I had no choice but to stick my head into the bowl and grab the pieces of bread with my lips.
It was humiliating and disgusting.
However, with smacking noises, I managed to take the bread piece by piece out of the bowl and slurp up the milk.
Both bowls weren't exactly full, but there was enough to satisfy the first big hunger.
As a precaution, I checked the bowls again to avoid a penalty. Luckily, this spectacle was over quickly and, feeling unsteady, I crawled out from

under the table and quickly left the kitchen. I quickly walked towards the basement stairs, curious about what would await me today.

As I walked down the stairs it got a little cooler than the rest of the apartment, but fortunately it was still pleasant so it wasn't cold.

With weak knees, I walked through the open door, along the red-lit narrow corridor into the main room. In the middle stood my master who looked at me without saying a word.

I was really happy to see him, especially in this room, of course, because that inner tingling feeling had arisen in me again since I was here again. The torment from just now had already been erased. So I didn't hesitate for a second and went to him to thank him for last night with a kiss. As I approached he held out his arm to keep me at a distance. Disappointed, I stopped and looked at him with questioning eyes.

"It made sense that you only got so little to eat today. Of course, you'll have an even richer meal later. Under the same circumstances, of course!" he said in a reassuring voice. In one hand he held a mouth ball which he put into my mouth without any further words and tied the leather strap behind my head.

A situation without words began again. I knew that I couldn't defend myself and that it would be pointless anyway. His body language was clear and I had to comply.

His hands felt over my body and examined it. He felt my neck, my shoulders, cupped my breasts, pinched my nipples through the thin material, stroked my stomach and my bottom. I didn't move and gave him free rein.

Finally he turned me and slipped off my panties and unclasped my bra.

With his fingers spread, he pressed my back lightly, which was the order for me to bend over. I took a deep breath through my nose and leaned forward as far as I could.

My master wasted no time and pulled my butt cheeks apart and then examined my anus with his finger. However, he was unable to penetrate, although he apparently had no intention of doing so. My labia were then pulled wide apart and examined.

Apparently everything was to his satisfaction and I was allowed to stand upright again. He turned me around again and looked deep into my eyes. His hand went between my legs. His gaze didn't leave mine as he expressionlessly began to rub my clitoris, driving my excitement further. Apart from the gentle smacking of my privates, there was complete silence that I could have endured for hours.

Finally he began to whisper sternly but quietly, "It's good that you're clean. That's what I expected. I'm going to have to give you a very large enema now and I expect you not to resist. Otherwise I will have to use educational measures."

My breath caught in my throat, but before I could think about it any further, my master grabbed me by the necklace and pulled me behind him towards the leather buck.

Without words and without gestures, he left me standing in front of the box and walked alone towards the bathroom.

As a matter of course, I supported my knees on the padding provided and leaned over the backrest so that my bottom was freely accessible to my master.

I waited quietly for him to return and meanwhile stared at the black wall that shimmered in the red neon light.

I quietly heard his footsteps and the rolling of the enema stand. His footsteps slowly became louder and louder until he finally stood behind me.

After a brief inspection, he adjusted my ankles and wrists and snapped the hinges attached to the padding shut. I was at the mercy again, helpless. I could literally feel my pussy getting wetter at the thought of how I would be tortured today.

My master gently slid his hand down my back to my anus. Since I was already prepared for the cool Vaseline, I wasn't shocked when he smeared it on my butthole. He did it very carefully and kept sliding two fingers into me to make everything slippery inside me.

He then slowly inserted the tube and the limp ball into me. I quickly noticed that he was inflating the ball more than normal. My anus was greatly stretched and tensed to the point of pain as the ball, fortunately, reached its maximum size. Even though I was a little more used to this strong stretch, it always felt strange to feel the blood pumping. But like everything, it had an extremely exciting aftertaste that I savored as much as possible.

Seconds later my master opened the valve and let the warm water flow into my intestines. Apparently the valve wasn't fully opened as the water seemed to flow quite slowly, so it took a while before I noticed the exciting feeling, which was by no means unpleasant. My stomach made a gurgling noise as the flow of water came to an end.

I remembered his last words that it was going to be a very big enema. If that was it, I could be proud of myself for taking the whole load so well.

Shortly afterwards I felt his hand on my spread bottom again, gently stroking it. "It's nice," he said, "that it worked out so well. "But you haven't made it yet." and gave me a hard slap on my left butt cheek with the flat of his hand.

I jumped, startled. It burned like hell and I could almost feel his hand red on my skin. Something was happening behind me, but unfortunately I couldn't see anything. Moments later, water began to flow into my intestines again. This time, however, it flowed faster and the pressure inside me increased quickly. Now I knew what to expect. A second bag was hanging on the enema stand! My stomach was already beginning to expand significantly, but the water continued to flow incessantly. Breathing deeply, I tried to stay relaxed and not tense up. I clearly noticed that my whole body was starting to sweat and millions of ants were crawling through my body.

Despite my gag, I tried to moan and show him that it was going too fast. However, apart from a quiet whimper, nothing left my filled mouth. Nevertheless, he seemed to know it and closed the valve slightly. The gurgling in my stomach was getting louder and the pressure was already becoming painful. Nevertheless, I tried to stay relaxed to make my master proud. Meanwhile he started to work on my dripping cunt with his hand. Drove two fingers deep into me and rubbed the slime on my buttocks. From the smell, there had to

be a lot leaking out of my lock. Suddenly the water stopped and tried in vain to let out a grateful purr. GOSSIP!
His flat hand hit my right butt cheek with a loud bang. The stabbing pain was deep and a tingling sensation seemed to spread throughout my entire body.
He grabbed my bottom with both hands and kneaded it vigorously several times, finishing with a light slap on the outside of my thighs.
"Did I do something wrong or why was he so rude to me?" it popped into my head. I had tried my hardest to be a good slave for him.
Suddenly my bonds were released and my master stood me up. I looked at him with sad eyes and hoped for a clarifying answer from him.
"Get up!" he ordered me in a stern voice.
With my stomach gurgling, I stood up carefully and tried to stand as straight as I could in front of him.
Apparently I had been sweating more than I thought, because my whole body seemed slightly shiny,
With a sarcastic grin, he looked at me from all sides and gently stroked my full stomach and my pelvis, which was stretched out backwards. My head was bowed submissively to show him my submission. After going around me once, he stood close in front of me. He lifted my head up and

began to lick the sweat from my neck with his tongue out. It seemed almost disgusting, but took it as a gentle caress and tried to show him by purring. Shortly afterwards my gag was released and he removed the ball from my mouth and I could finally breathe freely again.

"You seemed to like it, slave," and without warning pushed his hand between my legs.

"Your pussy slime is already running down your legs. Now, now. Lick it off, slave!", and held his wet hand in front of my face.

I carefully stuck out my tongue and licked up my juice. Of course I knew how I tasted, but this time I was forced, which I didn't particularly like. My Lord was right. I really must have been incredibly wet.

I quickly cleaned his hand of the slimy, salty secretion and then humbly lowered my head again.

He grabbed my collar and pulled me into the bathroom behind him. He positioned me quite quickly, loosened the enema ball and I was allowed to empty myself.

It took me quite a while to empty, and this time I found it particularly unpleasant. My bottom was still burning from his powerful blows and I had to sit on them, which didn't make things any more pleasant.

With a grumbling noise, my intestines were finally emptied and my master showered my abdomen with ice-cold water, which quickly alleviated the pain. After drying off, he walked with me into the main room and walked straight towards the flat, straight bench.

He motioned for me to take a seat there, which I did immediately. He pushed my upper body down and pulled me forward so that my legs could dangle relaxed. He led my arms back over my head where my wrists were tied like it was usual for a stretching bench. My legs remained loose and were just spread wide, but I had already gotten used to that. From somewhere below he brought out a kind of pillow, which he pushed under my back so that I had to arch my back.

He examined me again and dug two nipple clamps out of his pocket. He twisted my nipples vigorously with his fingers, causing them to become erect. A biting pain shot through my chest as the first clamp bit, and another pain followed the second clamp pinching my nipple.

The stabbing pain continued to spread and turned into a dull numbness. I curiously raised my head to see what followed. My master opened his pants and took out his hard cock. He finally took off his pants completely and stood between my spread legs. I tried to relax, closing my eyes and tilting my head back, but that didn't ease the pain in my nipples.

And there he was.

He purposefully guided his bulging glans over my clitoris, through my labia and then pushed hard into my dripping cunt. My breath was taken away and I let out a shrill groan. He sank his full length into me and began to take me hard. The smacking sound as his cock left my core was unmistakable. Even though he kept thrusting very hard, it made me forget the biting nipple pain. His hard cock really filled me up and stretched my insides further with every thrust. His veiny shaft rubbed hard against my labia and after a few more thrusts a lightning bolt shot through me and goosebumps covered my body.

He must have noticed how my body jerked because he slowed down and let his cock slide into me more easily. All the way in and out of me. It was an exhilarating feeling.

But before I could continue enjoying his cock, he suddenly pulled it out of my dripping cunt. He walked around the bench and grabbed my head firmly, practically pressing it onto his slippery cock. He pushed it so fast and deep into me that I almost had to gag. And before I could react, his hot sperm shot down my throat. I couldn't help myself and swallowed his seed. His cock was still pulsating into my mouth, which was covered all over with his sperm.

Luckily I managed to swallow the entire mass of sperm without spilling.

Grinning, my master finally pulled it out of my mouth, which made me feel freer again and was able to lick the greasy semen from the roof of my mouth.

The biting pinch in my nipples became noticeable again, I internally hoped that the painful clamps would now be removed. But nothing happened.

"You have done well, slave. I will reward you in my own way."

With these words he roughly pulled me up by the chain and dragged me to the St. Andrew's Cross.

The nipple clamps now pulled down even more painfully and seemed to almost bite through my nipples.

When I got to the cross, I stood on the cross despite the pain.

However, my master wanted it the other way around and turned me so that my back was to him and then had me tied up hand and foot.

After examining my body again, he went to the cupboards and dug something out. My master knelt down and stretched my labia. Now it was clear to me what he must have in his hand. Luckily for me, they were padded brackets that were only equipped with weights. I clearly noticed a slight pinch on my labia and how the weight pulled them downwards. Luckily it wasn't that painful, I found the idea of my lips hanging down and stretched out much worse. But as almost always, I had no other choice, after all my body belonged to my master, who decided everything.

My Lord disappeared again, leaving me helpless on the cross. It took a while until he came back with a box in his hand. The first thing he took out of the box was the ball for the mouth. He pushed it deep into my mouth and closed it. My jaw had just gotten used to normal conditions again and was now wide open again. A feeling I didn't want to get used to.

An uneasy feeling plagued me from then on. Nothing happened for a while. No touching, no torture.

My knees felt weak and I struggled to stay upright. After all, when my master was watching me, I wanted to stand proud and upright, as befits a slave.

It was definitely over 15 minutes in which nothing happened. I heard footsteps coming towards me again, getting closer and closer.

GOSSIP! Without warning, a leather strap hit me on my left butt cheek. The searing pain made me wince. The blow was damn hard and masked all other pain.

GOSSIP! The strap hit my other butt cheek. I winced again. I couldn't defend myself or escape the torture. Only a whimper left my mouth.

The burning pain shot through my entire pelvis. My master ran the leather strap down my back, causing my body to tremble.

The blows were very hard and I had no idea why he hit me.

The burning sensation from the butt slaps faded slightly and became a strangely exciting tingling sensation.

The leather strap of the crop was now on my bottom and continued down between my legs and along the inside of my thighs. Goosebumps followed the strap, further increasing the tingling sensation. When he reached my ankle, he moved up again, lightly hitting my inner thigh alternately. Once at the top, he guided the leather strap onto my clamped cunt and stroked it. I became more and more excited and could literally feel my softness running down my elongated labia and collecting on the round weights. He led the leather strap back again and stroked it over my anus several times. I groaned as much as I could.

"Seems you like this too, slave. However, you're acting like a bitch!"
GOSSIP! A hard blow hit me on the bottom.
GOSSIP! SMACK Two more followed.
It hurt and I couldn't hold back the tears.
What had I done wrong?
The sharp pain disappeared again and excited me even more. I felt like I was on a roller coaster. Pain and pleasure dominated my thoughts and my helpless situation only made it worse.
There was a pause. I breathed deeply in and out through my nose and tried to sort out my thoughts.
Suddenly there was something very cold on my bottom. Something wet and cold. It traveled from my butt crack down to my anus. I had no idea what that was. It was hard and cold. My master moved it over my butt hole several times and finally to my pussy hole.
US!
It had to be ice, the way it felt. It was uncomfortably cold and damp.
He came closer and closer to my hole with the ice rod and finally penetrated deep into my wet pussy.
The cold quickly spread throughout my body. Within seconds my abdomen felt numb. The cold was extremely unpleasant and made me shiver. It had to be a very thick ice stick. Thicker than my

master's cock. After he inserted the rod all the way into me, I noticed that it became thicker towards the end and stretched my entrance very wide. After it couldn't go any further, he pulled the cold rod out of me again and went back to my anus.

With pressure he pushed against my closed butthole, which routinely opened. The numbness of the cold set in again. But the rod dug deeper and deeper into my gut, spreading a terrible cold. My initial pleasure turned into unpleasant trembling.

My bottom stretched further and further and took in the slippery ice stick.

My master had to push harder and harder to get the ice rod into me. When things couldn't go any further, the rod was slowly removed again. But the cold remained.

After a short pause in which the cold gave way to my body heat, the process was repeated. Once again the ice made its way between the dangling weights on my labia and then pushed back into my gaping cunt.

This time my master moved faster and began thrusting the rod back and forth. The unpleasant cold increased again, making my body shiver.

He slowly started to fuck me deep with the ice. However, my desire did not return. The ice was too

thick and stretched me, and the growing cold it gave off was too uncomfortable.
With each thrust he pushed the ice a little deeper and stretched my hole to the limit.
I tried to beg for mercy. The ice was too thick and the cold caused my abdomen to convulse. But as usual, the ball sat too deep in my mouth so that only distorted sounds could be heard.
But he seemed to have heard and shortly afterwards ended his icy torture.
It seemed like it took an eternity for my abdomen to warm up again, but I was absolutely happy.
My mouth gag was released and my bonds were opened. I struggled to stay on my feet

Monday:
The warming touch of the morning sun brought me out of my pleasant sleep and painfully reminded me that I was alone in the huge marital bed.
My master had quietly left during the night. As usual, he disappeared silently without leaving a final message or anything, let alone waking me up when he left the house.
My eyes slowly opened and I adjusted to the bright morning sun that filled the bedroom with a warm atmosphere.
As I was ordered, nothing covered my body.

No nightgown, no underwear.
My body needed a few minutes to awaken all its strength and then give me the energy to get up.
A final stretch and stretch ended my wake-up procedure and I disappeared into the bathroom.
The morning shower wouldn't have been necessary; The night had hardly left any traces on me. Only a little wetness had collected between my legs. But even if my master wasn't present, I obviously wanted to take care of myself and make myself look pretty.
Despite the incredible satisfaction I felt last evening, I couldn't stop myself from masturbating in the shower. I would have loved to let my master take me through last night.
My two fingers did little to help.
After washing myself completely and throwing on the silky dressing gown, I made my way to the mailbox. Even if in all probability only bills or advertising awaited me, that would at least keep me busy for a while and relieve me of the boredom that would await me that day.
I would be reluctant to describe my life as living in a golden cage, even though it often seems like it.
Most of the day, there is nothing too great to do.
Clean up a bit, read something and occasionally go shopping.

But living without worries is ultimately also a desirable way to eke out an existence.

I opened the massive wooden door of our house and unlocked the mailbox hanging next to it. The first thing that fell into my hands was a heavy white A4 envelope, with only a small normal letter fluttering behind it.

A little taken aback, I went back into the house, sat at the kitchen table and looked at what I had stolen.

At first I thought it was a thick mail order catalog, but then the address wouldn't say SLAVE. A little scared, but still curious, I excitedly opened the envelope and pulled out the contents. There were two stapled pads of paper and a single letter:

Good morning slave,

Since I, your master, cannot educate you in the near future, I will entrust you to yourself.

You will find out everything you need in the enclosed documents. Always complete your tasks conscientiously and honorably.

My eye will constantly watch over you.

You will have visitors on Thursday. You will serve him faithfully, just as you serve me.

The visitor has all the rights that I have, which means that you will submit to him as you do to me.

Make no distinction between Me and your visit!
Complete your tasks and submit to your destiny as my slave.
Your Lord

I was both scared and curious. I put the letter aside and took the remaining documents out of the envelope.

SLAVE TEACHING - was written in bold letters above the first pad. Not yet suspecting anything bad, I turned the first page of the thick booklet and landed straight into the first chapter - Rules of a Slave Girl.

But before I started reading any further, I made the long-awaited coffee and prepared something to eat. A few slices were quickly made and the coffee was ready.

I eagerly started reading:

Rule 1: I serve and obey my Lord.

"That was obvious to me," I said to myself, "I don't need a set of rules for that."

But it went further and I followed the lines, rule by rule, full of inner tension.

Rule 6: I am an object of my master. My body and my mind are the property of my Lord.

I gulped while reading the 6th rule. I didn't want to be defined as an "object." After all, I was a responsible, mature woman. Much more than an object.

However, when I thought about my past experiences, it became clear relatively quickly that I was allowing myself to be treated like an object. And I enjoyed it too, even if the feelings were quite bizarre.

Rule 8: I set aside my own will and accept the wishes, views and goals of my Lord.
Rule 16: The Lord is free to punish me as he pleases.
Rule 21: My body is the most important gift I can give to my Lord. I give him my body as his property.
The more I read, the closer I came to realizing that my life was about to take a decisive turn. And apparently I had no choice in this lifestyle.
Rule 23: I know that my body is weak and my Lord will show me my limits again and again. I will do everything I can to push these boundaries as far as possible in order to better correspond to my master's ideas.
Rule 29: My vagina is the womb of my sexuality. I make sure that the labia minora and the clitoris foreskin are visible in the presence of my master. If necessary, I ask my Lord to be allowed to bring her into this state himself.

Rule 56: As a slave, I always behave in such a way that my master is proud of me in the presence of other masters, mistresses, slaves or slaves.

Rule 57: Should my master deem fit to lend me to another master or mistress, I will be a slave to him or her to the same extent as to my master.

Rule 66: I thank my master for every punishment on me, as it allows me to become an even better slave.

Rule 70: I will never ask for a remission of a punishment or a relief from a punishment for any reason whatsoever.

I swallowed deeply after going through my rule book. These should be the rules for my new life? 70 perfectly thought out rules that would dictate my life from now on. This system no longer allowed me to live the way I had previously led it.

Just as I was frightened, I felt a deep tingling sensation inside me that clearly said that I would enjoy my life as a slave.

I liked the idea and even if it was a difficult and rocky road, I would want to endure it.

But the block was far from over.

The second part followed;

- The slaveholdings

Another incredible system of postures for all occasions and occasions was presented to me.

Completely spellbound and fascinated, I memorized everything as precisely as possible. The basic submissive postures, the punishing postures, everything.

After all, it would guide the rest of my life. Besides, I didn't want to disappoint and embarrass my master when he returned. Who knows what he'll have in store when he comes back. I still remembered the rules about dealing with other slaves and mistresses. I secretly hoped that something like that would never cross his mind. Because if there was one thing that disgusted me, it was same-sex sex or something similar.

When I went to put the rules back in the envelope, I almost missed a small piece of paper.

Surprised, I dug it out of the envelope and read:

Tasks

, so you don't get too bored while I'm away. I hope that you adhere to them strictly and improve yourself accordingly.

I demand that you stretch your labia several times a day so that they lengthen significantly.

I demand that you stretch your pussy several times a day. You're already a little dilated, but I wish you were a lot more dilated. I wish that when I return I can sink my fist into you.

I require that you stretch your butthole in the same way several times a day.

In order to carry out these tasks, I have stored a suitcase under the bed that contains all the necessary tools.

I want you to walk around "freely" as little as possible!

I know what I ask of you and I give you respect!

Complete your tasks diligently and I will reward you with pride.

Your Lord

I had to swallow hard to get rid of the lump in my throat.

What my master asked of me there was really awesome. What woman wants to look used and worn out? And at my age too. At 33 you shouldn't look THAT way. I also thought that I looked too used. After all, the ordeals quickly left their mark.

But now it was my job and I didn't even dare to imagine opposing my master's tasks.

Despite my inner reluctance, I eagerly went into the bedroom.

In order to follow the rules straight away, I took off my dressing gown and put on my slave collar. No one could see me, but the collar still had its effect on me.

Although all the heaters were running at the highest level so that I wouldn't freeze even naked,

it was clear to me that it wasn't the heater that was making me sweat.
Trembling with tension, I leaned down and pulled the suitcase from under the bed.
He didn't seem to be too heavy and hoped that my tasks would be easier than I imagined.
Excitedly, I opened the zipper and opened it.
I looked into a chaos of devices, which didn't ease my tension.
Somehow I had to get an overview and started by emptying the suitcase.
I neatly lined up all the things in front of the bed. There were tons of different sized dildos and plugs, many of which I already knew all too well. The two labia clamps with many different weights were of course also there. A few interesting looking things like a ball chain and love balls were also present. Last but not least, a very large bottle of lubricant was added to the smorgasbord.
Despite the sometimes frightening looking things, I clearly noticed that I was already getting more and more wet.
True to my duties, I grabbed some less threatening objects and squatted on the end of the bed so that I could see myself in the mirrored closet doors.
I slowly let my gaze wander over my exposed body. Spread my legs a little. looked at my inner sanctum

and opened it slightly with my fingers. Shaking my head, I thought again about my master's wishes.

Finally I took the studded love balls. I slowly rubbed them between my labia with light pressure to moisten them. A pleasant warmth spread and I pushed the first ball into my pussy. I clearly felt the pressure she was exerting. Nevertheless, it wasn't unpleasant and after a few moments the second one followed. Pleasant tingling spread across my entire abdomen, even though the balls weren't moving.

First I took the time and enjoyed the beautiful feeling when I tugged on the white ribbon that peeped out of me.

However, I could literally feel my master's punitive look if he saw me neglecting his request.

I mentally admonished myself and reached for the plug that was intended for my bottom. Unfortunately my master hadn't packed the smaller ones in his suitcase, but the smallest black one still made a pleasant impression.

Without being sparing, I rubbed him with the lubricant and placed him on the floor with his relatively large foot. I generously lubricated my asshole with the remaining gel and knelt on the floor in front of the plug.

I slowly lowered my pelvis and felt the tip of the plug opening my butt hole. I got closer and closer to the thickest part, when I reached it, the plug slipped completely into my butt and sucked itself into me.

In the mirror I saw the eyes of a completely corrupt woman; a bondage slave.

I now clearly noticed the pressure inside me as I slowly stood up. I hadn't yet taken my eyes off my reflection. If you only saw my head, you could think I was a really decent, sensible woman. Beautiful fair skin, but still had slight red welts in some places.

A delicate figure, but marked by sweet torture. And a once equally delicate abdomen that was now corrupted by shameful deeds.

I quickly ended my thoughts and prepared for the next task. I took a deep breath and reached for the labia clamps.

I straightened my little lips, which were already no longer little, and attached both clamps. There were no weights hanging on it yet.

Since my master aroused a certain ambition in me with his demands, I chose the weights a little bolder and carefully hung them on the brackets.

At first it was a bit tugging, but my skin was apparently more elastic than I thought.

As I stood and took the first steps, I clearly felt how the "innards" were defending their place. Still,

it wasn't particularly unpleasant and the added ambition made up for any doubts.
The housework was already waiting for me in the kitchen. When I got to the bottom I was already very annoyed by the hanging, which made walking quite annoying. Not only did it dangle back and forth with every step, the walking also caused the weights to pull on my lips more than if I stood still. Apparently I had no choice but to endure it and I set about dealing with the dirty dishes and the dust.
After about half an hour I was finished with everything. Done with your homework and your nerves. Because not only did the weights move with every step, the love balls also moved. After this short time I was sweating wetly and literally shaking with excitement. I suspected that my master wouldn't think it right if I gave in to my lust now, but I had no other choice at that moment. I had to get rid of my inner tension at all costs.
I quickly went into the bedroom and lay down on the bed.
I lay on my back and carefully pulled on the clamps until the slight pain came. My Lord would certainly do the same.
Finally, I released the clamps and gave all my attention to the white ribbon peeking out of my wet pussy.

I pulled on it slowly and enjoyed the intense tickle the nubs gave me. For every millimeter the balls traveled, my body thanked me with pure pleasure. Beads of sweat ran down my temple as I got closer to orgasm.

It was almost time. The balls slipped out and my abdomen released all its strength and, panting, I enjoyed thrust after thrust as my pussy unloaded. It truly was a wonderful orgasm, as if I hadn't had one in weeks.

My asshole tried with all its might to fight against the plug, but in vain. I lay in bed bathed in sweat for a long minute and enjoyed the wonderful feeling.

What I urgently needed now was a shower. Said and done. I grabbed a bigger dildo and took a shower. Finally, my master asked me to stretch as often as I could.

Seconds later, warm water splashed over my body. I was quickly soaped up and quickly got to work filling myself up again.

The plug in my butt still fit perfectly, but my still glowing hole was literally hungry for something. While I no longer felt any desire, my feelings were ultimately a low priority. I had internalized that by now.

I leaned against the tiles and opened my legs slightly. I applied the blunt tip and pushed it bit by

bit into my spoiled hole. It was a bit tight now, even though it wasn't the biggest thing in the suitcase. But even if slowly, it finally fit and together with the plug I was really completely filled.
There were several straps at the bottom of the shaft so I could strap it around myself to keep it in place.
I turned off the water and dried myself off in peace. Even the first steps out of the bathroom were difficult and I visibly had to walk with my legs apart, which made it very uncomfortable.
Once I got to the bedroom I decided I didn't want to move around too much to keep it as comfortable as possible. I knew that when my master was back, he would scare me enough. And so I chose the lesser evil and more or less hobbled down to the living room and grabbed a book.
Lying comfortably on the couch, the time passed quickly while reading and if my rumbling stomach hadn't bothered me, I would definitely have continued lazing around until the evening.
My excitement was limited the whole time because I barely moved.
But now it was time again.
Off to the kitchen.
The thickly veined stick was secure and its size became more and more problematic during

cooking. My abdomen kept trying in vain to fight the pressure. I seemed to feel every single vein and even though it didn't hurt particularly, I wanted nothing more than to get rid of it.
The noodles with tofu were quickly devoured as quickly as they were made. I'm not a fan of complicated dishes. It should be quick and easy. After all, my master doesn't want to have a block. The pressure inside me was getting stronger from my full stomach and I finally deserved a break. While I was still on the kitchen chair, I opened the buckles, took a deep breath and slowly pulled the dildo out. It was truly a tremendous relief and the greatest burden was lifted.
But my butt hole should also be allowed to recover and, leaning against the worktop with my chest, I pulled out the plug. The wonderful feeling dominated and drove away the burning sensation on my bottom. Apparently the gel had evaporated a bit during the shower and so he sat a little dry. But this incredible feeling of liberation was soothing enough.
Cleaning the dishes was now more than just a relief.
It was already afternoon and time was moving faster than I would have liked.
But I had mastered my tasks and enjoyed my book with a clear conscience.

The rest of the day was routine. Do some chores, dinner and finally get ready for bed.
After I took a shower shortly before going to sleep, I rinsed the last remaining lubricant out of my butt. Even these little enemas with the balloon were still uncomfortable for me. But what does it have to do?
However, I treated myself to one last look in the mirror before going to bed.
There was no longer any sign of the morning's exertions. My butt hole no longer burned and only my labia were still a little red.
I opened my pussy a little with two fingers and seriously considered whether my master wasn't asking too much of me. After all, one fist was even bigger than the dildo this afternoon.
But I had no choice but to trust him and prepare myself for it.
As I looked at myself in the mirror, the initial tingling sensation began and I wished my Lord was with me and would still it. But I was simply too tired to lend a hand. I crawled into bed and closed my eyes.
The end of a successful day

About the Author

Maria Valleetsy